27,95

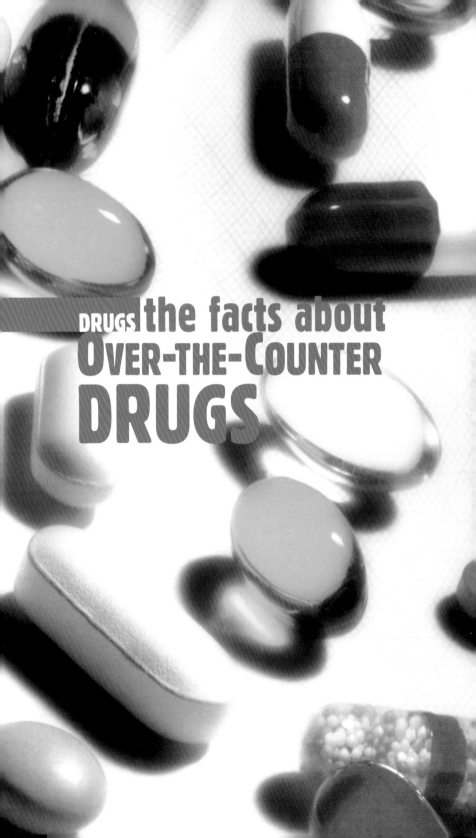

DRUGS the facts about
OVER-THE-COUNTER
DRUGS

DRUGS the facts about
OVER-THE-COUNTER
DRUGS

LORRIE KLOSTERMAN

Marshall Cavendish
Benchmark
New York

This book is dedicated to Carol, whose generous friendship cures so much!

Acknowledgment:
Thanks to John Roll, Ph.D., director of Behavioral Pharmacology at UCLA Integrated Substance
Abuse Programs, for his expert review of this manuscript.

Marshall Cavendish Benchmark
99 White Plains Road
Tarrytown, NY 10591
www.marshallcavendish.us

Library of Congress Cataloging-in-Publication Data

Klosterman, Lorrie.
The facts about over-the-counter drugs / by Lorrie Klosterman.
p. cm. — (Drugs)

Includes bibliographical references and index.
ISBN-13: 978-0-7614-2246-4
ISBN-10: 0-7614-2246-3
1. Drugs. 2. Drugs--Safety measures. 3. Pediatric pharmacology.
I. Title. II. Series: Drugs (Benchmark Books (Firm))

RJ560.K475 2006
615'.1--dc22
2005037349

Photo Research by Joan Meisel

Cover photo: Herrmann Starke/Corbis
Alamy: 12, David R. Frazier Photolibrary; 44, Brand X Pictures; Corbis:
1, 2–3, 5, Herrmann Starke; 18, Images.com; 20, DK Limited; 25; 33,
Randy Duchaine; 37, Mediscan; 64, Chuck Savage; 70, Kimberly White;
Courtesy of the FDA: 26; Peter Arnold, Inc.: 6, SIU; 54, Leonard
Lessin; 79, Matt Meadows.

Printed in China
1 3 5 6 4 2

Juv
615
Klefa

CONTENTS

THE VAST ARRAY OF OVER-THE-COUNTER DRUGS CAN BE DIZZYING WHEN YOU
HAVE TO CHOOSE ONE TO HELP WITH ANY OF THE VARIOUS MALADIES THAT
MIGHT NOT REQUIRE PRESCRIPTION MEDICATIONS. THIS IS JUST A SMALL
SELECTION OF PAIN RELIEVERS AVAILABLE IN MOST STORES.

1 What Are Over-the-Counter Drugs?

Over-the-counter drugs are a vast assortment of substances used to treat or prevent common ailments. A stroll down the aisles of a supermarket or pharmacy reveals an amazing diversity and abundance of these products. Pain relievers, cold and flu remedies, hay fever medicines, itch relievers, antibacterial creams, acne treatments, antiperspirants, dandruff shampoos, and sunscreens are just some of the more familiar varieties. These medications are sold as pills, liquids, wafers, gums, pastes, lotions, oils, gels, sprays, powders, or patches to put on the skin. Some are inhaled into the airways.

More than ever, people rely on finding aid from the drugstore or supermarket shelf. Many of these products bring relief to annoying and debilitating symptoms. In addition, over-the-counter (OTC) medicines allow people to treat minor ailments without consulting a doctor. This do-it-yourself approach is becoming more popular as the cost of health insurance increases and becomes too expensive for some people to afford. Without insurance to cover the cost of a doctor visit or prescription medicines, people are turning to self-treatment with OTC products as the only affordable option. Besides, many health ailments are minor and short-lived, and don't warrant a visit to a doctor.

Altogether, one can choose from thousands of over-the-counter items in more than eighty different categories. They are available not just in drug-stores but virtually anywhere, from the huge superstores that sell almost everything to the smallest convenience stores. And they appear in vending machines at rest stops along major highways, in airports, and in college buildings.

This remarkable abundance and widespread availability of OTC products does more than please consumers. Manufacturers of these products profit greatly from their sale. Consumers in the United States collectively spend many billions of dollars each year on them. But some health experts are concerned that people have become all too eager to "pop a pill" to deal with minor problems that would go away on their own, or could be treated by nondrug approaches. Over-the-counter products make taking a pill (or using a syrup, lotion, cream, or spray) very easy. And manufacturers of those products encourage our eagerness to do so. The sheer number of OTC products, and the massive advertising campaigns that promote them, are a constant suggestion that the body needs lots of help to stay healthy or to recover from illnesses. Yet, in the vast majority of cases, our bodies are able to heal on their own, given time, rest, and good nutrition.

Of course, many over-the-counter drugs do a great service by relieving the discomfort of symptoms such as fever and aches of the flu, annoying itchiness of skin rashes and bug bites, cramps of digestive turmoil, pain of pulled muscles, and so on. They also allow people to continue to meet life's demands as though everything were fine. That has its drawbacks, however. An illness that is ignored by covering up its symptoms can get worse or evolve into multiple health problems. And continuing to go to school or work while sick might impress the teacher or the boss—until the illness spreads to others.

What's in a Word: Drugs, Medicines, and Products
It is helpful to explain some words that are used when talking about over-the-counter substances. One is the word *drug*. Some people use *drug* in a very strict sense to mean only those substances that are abused and usually obtained illegally, such as heroin or cocaine, and use *medicine* or *medication* to mean the substances that are intended to help with a medical condition. Drug manufacturers often use

9

medicine or *medication* when advertising their products because those words sound more inviting than *drug*.

However, many people use *drug* to refer to any substance the body does not naturally make, and which is designed to have some impact on how a person's body functions. That usage includes both over-the-counter substances and those available only through a doctor's prescription. The federal government uses that definition when it makes decisions about products that are for sale to the public. This book will follow that usage. Even though over-the-counter products are such a common part of modern life that it may seem strange to think of them as drugs, they are.

Then there is the idea of a drug *product*. That phrase means anything containing a drug. Some drug products have lots of nondrug substances that make them more appealing, such as flavorings, colorings, and fragrances. Other nondrug substances create a desired consistency for the product, making it a gel, paste, lotion, or syrup. In addition, some products contain not just a single drug, but several, each with its own purpose. For example, the products that help relieve symptoms of a cold or flu, such as Children's Tylenol Cold Plus Cough Multi Symptom Liquid, have so many ingredients they can't be referred to as a single drug. Their names often are a clue to their complex mixture of ingredients.

Of course, there are products that are very simple. For instance, pain-relieving drugs often come as pills (tablets), containing a certain amount of a single drug plus enough nondrug material (such as xanthanum gum) to hold the pill together. A pill that is meant to be swallowed usually is also coated with a thin shell to be sure it doesn't dissolve in the mouth, or the drug may come as a powder in a gelatin capsule. Chewable pills contain flavorings and sweeteners. Each of these simple "products" may be referred to by the drug name, such as acetaminophen. Or, since drug names often are tongue-twisters, people might refer to a drug manufacturer's name for the drug. For example, Tylenol is one manufacturer's name for a product that contains acetaminophen.

Over-the-Counter, or Behind It?
In the United States, certain drugs can only be obtained legally with a doctor's permission. That permission is written by the doctor in a note called a prescription. Prescriptions are meant to ensure that a person who is going to be taking a drug has actually seen a doctor face-to-face, so the doctor can properly check the person's condition. The person then takes the doctor's note to a pharmacist, who "fills" the prescription, which means to measure out the amount of drug the doctor recommended, such as a two-week supply of pills.

Using or selling prescription drugs without a doctor's permission is illegal because those kinds of drugs are very strong and have potentially harmful effects on the body. Some are highly addictive.

IF A PERSON IS CONFUSED ABOUT WHICH OVER-THE-COUNTER MEDICINE TO CHOOSE, IT IS WISE TO CONSULT A PHARMACIST BEFORE BUYING.

Some can be deadly when used improperly. The intent of that law is to make sure that only a person who really needs that sort of drug for a medical condition is using it, and is working with a doctor to do so safely.

Over-the-counter drugs, on the other hand, are stocked on shelves where anyone, of any age, may buy them. They are not kept locked away behind the pharmacist's counter but instead are "over the counter." But that doesn't mean they are harmless. As drugs, they have an effect, and in some people those effects are dangerous.

So what distinguishes over-the-counter drugs from prescription drugs? The following are characteristics of over-the-counter drugs and products that set them apart from prescription drugs—at least in most cases. There can be exceptions.

- The possible dangers of taking OTC drugs are mild or happen infrequently—as long as people take them as directed.
- The possibility of harm to a person's health is very low compared to the benefits in using the drug or drug product.
- The consumer can figure out which product is the right one to take, out of the many products available, by reading and comparing labels.
- The proper manner of taking OTC products can be well explained on a label (rather than requiring a doctor's or a pharmacist's explanation).
- OTC drugs are not as likely to be abused as some prescription drugs because they either are not addictive, or, if they are, are present in amounts too small to cause addiction when used as directed.
- OTC drugs are often, though not always, less expensive than prescription drugs.

There are cases where those generalizations aren't true. Sometimes an over-the-counter product does more harm to a person than good. For example, a person might have a serious allergic reaction to an OTC drug or nondrug ingredient. Or, an

OTC drug that is considered safe when taken for a few days at a time may be harmful if taken more often, yet no one is stopping the consumer from taking it as often as he or she wants to. (Prescriptions limit a person's supply.)

What's more, OTC products can be dangerous because people are in charge of their own drug-taking, and they make mistakes. They sometimes misread the label, don't read it thoroughly, or don't bother to read it at all. They might then take a dangerous amount of the drug or take it when other substances (including other drugs) are in their bloodstream, with serious, even fatal, consequences. Young children sometimes mistake pills for candy and liquid drug products for juice, and will consume a life-threatening dose if the container is open and within reach. Iron-containing vitamins, for example, fatally poisoned nearly forty children under the age of three in the United States between 1986 and 1994.

Of course, many of the potential dangers of OTC drugs are also true of prescription drugs. But because OTC products are so readily available, consumers often assume there are no risks in taking them. It is important to remember that using any drug, whether prescription or OTC, carries some level of risk.

Prescription or OTC: Who Decides?
Who decides if a drug may be sold over the counter or by prescription only? In the United States, it is

14

the Food and Drug Administration (FDA), which is an agency of the federal government. Within the FDA, there is a group known as the Center for Drug Evaluation and Research (CDER), whose jobs include making sure OTC products are safe and properly labeled. It reviews new products and must give the "okay" to the company that makes them before those products can be put out on store shelves and sold to the public.

CDER also collects information about problems people are having with both OTC and prescription drugs that are being sold already, although there has been criticism by consumer safety organizations, journalists, and some doctors and health experts that CDER doesn't do much with that information. Also, doctors and drug companies are supposed to report to CDER problems that people are having with prescription drugs, but not with OTC drugs. However, people can call, write, or e-mail CDER directly about problems they are having with OTC products. Then, if many people are having trouble with a drug, the government may force the manufacturer to add warnings to the label, or change the dosage instructions, or remove it from over-the-counter sales altogether.

Some drugs may become prescription-only after that, or be taken off the market. An example is the drug phenylpropanolamine, once an ingredient in dozens of OTC nasal decongestants and weight-control products. In 2000, the FDA and CDER asked drug companies to stop using it because a study had

15

just shown that more women using those products were having strokes (serious bleeding around the brain) than women who weren't using them.

Sometimes a prescription drug will be switched into the category of an OTC drug. So instead of getting it only with a doctor's permission and from "behind the counter" at the pharmacy, the drug (or product) becomes available to anybody. A switch happens when CDER is convinced that enough studies have proved the product safe for the general public, or when it has been used safely by enough people for a long time without any (or rarely any) serious problems. Hundreds of the OTC products on the shelves today are there because of the prescription-to-OTC switching process. Some people believe this is not a good idea. In fact, some health experts and consumer protection groups are quick to point out that all drugs carry a danger, all the more so when made freely available to the public, which may ignore directions. They also worry that the safety tests haven't been thorough enough to put some of those drugs out into the general public. But with drug manufacturers eager to sell products, and consumers eager to try them, there is a lot of impetus for getting drugs out from behind the pharmacist's counter.

Brand Names, Drug Names, and Generics
Large drugstores and grocery stores have shelves and shelves of over-the-counter products. There are

so many to choose from that it can be overwhelming to figure out what product to buy. Fortunately, products are usually organized into sections according to what they are used for. All the different kinds of cold remedies are grouped together, all the itch relievers are together, and so on. Even so, there can be dozens of similar-sounding, similar-looking items to choose from. How does one decide which to buy?

One thing people sometimes look for is a brand they recognize. A drug manufacturing company creates a *brand*—a unique name, logo, and color scheme—that it prints on the packaging of its products. Some well-known brand names in the pain-reliever category are Bayer, Tylenol, Excedrin, and Advil. But often, next to these brand-name products, are rather plain-looking ones—the *generic* versions. Those don't usually have fancy names, but instead might simply list a drug name on the package and the name of the store that's selling the product, and perhaps the store's logo. What are these generic forms, and where do they come from?

A generic drug product is identical to a brand-name product whose patent protection has expired. Patent protection means that for twenty years after a new drug is created by a drug company, nobody else can legally make and sell that drug (or product). However, after that time has passed, anyone can make and sell it. Drug products with generic matches are those that are no longer under patent protection—their patents have expired. Large

WHAT'S THE DIFFERENCE BETWEEN A BRAND NAME AND A GENERIC DRUG? FAMILIARITY AND—PRICE. NAME BRANDS COST MORE.

drugstores offer their own generic versions of many popular brand-name products, from the simplest single-drug items to the more complicated, multi-drug elixirs.

Are generic drugs as good as brand-name drugs? Yes. Generic drugs are made under the same regulations and safety requirements as brand-name drugs. Each generic product is required by law to be as strong, as pure, and of the same quality as an existing product. For example, one pill of Benadryl

Allergy Relief (a brand-name product) might contain twenty-five milligrams of diphenhydramine hydrochloride, an antihistamine. A generic product might be called "Allergy Relief" and have the store's name and/or logo on it, and would contain the same drug in the same amount per pill. The colorings, flavorings, and other inert ingredients may be different, though. The main difference between brand-name and generic drug products is that generics cost less.

So why doesn't everyone buy generic products if they are available? Advertising power. People become convinced through ads that certain brands are the best. In fact, one of the main purposes of advertising is to get people to recognize a brand when they see it on the shelf, remember how great it seemed in the ad, and buy it. In addition, people tend to trust a product they recognize by brand name and have used for years, before a generic version became available.

Over-the-counter drug products are flourishing, with generics crowding the shelves next to myriad brand-name products, and the prescription-to-OTC switch process contributing a steady influx of new drugs to the OTC line-up. Fortunately, these products have some hoops to jump through that popular remedies a century ago didn't have to—hoops that ensure they will be safer and effective. OTC products still are not foolproof or perfect, but they've come a long way.

NATIVE AMERICANS HAVE LONG HAD A TRADITION OF HEALING BY HERBS, INCLUDING SUCH STIMULANT AND RELAXANT HERBS AS BLACK ROOT, INDIAN TOBACCO, AND BLACK COHOSH, PICTURED HERE.

2 A HISTORY OF DRUG PRODUCTS IN THE UNITED STATES

Long before chemists began to extract compounds out of plants and test them as medicines, and before the advent of the huge drug manufacturing companies that exist today, people treated ailments and illnesses with remedies they made themselves. Our distant ancestors figured out—presumably by trial and error—which plants, minerals, and combinations thereof were useful for what sorts of ailments. The recipes for these so-called folk remedies, or home remedies, were passed on by word of mouth from generation to generation. Some of them may not have really done much good, but some certainly did. Today, few people remember them, though a renewed interest in natural, homemade remedies is growing; some of those recipes were the basis for OTC or prescription drugs.

The transition from a society that relied on folk remedies to one that now offers hundreds of manufactured drug products has been gradual, reaching all the way back to colonial times. The first settlers carried knowledge of folk remedies across the seas from settlers' homelands, though the plant ingredients they needed didn't necessarily grow in the New World. New recipes had to be worked out, or ingredients imported. Of course, Native peoples in the New World had their own rich knowledge of healing, but the colonists' European heritage had a stronger influence on how medicines and drug products evolved. And there were clever individuals who quickly realized that the colonies were a wide-open market for selling manufactured medicines like those already popular in Europe—mysterious concoctions that often promised miracle cures, but sometimes injured people instead or, occasionally, killed them.

These early medicines—called potions, elixirs, remedies, nostrums, tonics, liniments, ointments, and so on—were largely created to make money. Some really did help with certain symptoms, though many did not. They might have created a noticeable change in a person's body, but in ways that didn't have anything to do with a particular illness. For instance, alcohol was a popular ingredient. It probably had little effect on specific health problems, but it made people feel different, that's for sure! Some potions actually contained toxic, injurious, or highly addictive substances such as morphine, heroin, or cocaine. It was common for people to be sickened, permanently maimed, or sometimes even killed by these "medicines." People had to use them at their own risk. And if something horrific happened to them, the salesman might be long gone, never to be seen again.

One of our most respected presidents, Abraham Lincoln, took a common remedy known as "the blue mass," which contained mercury, as an aid for depression (then called melancholia). In 2001 a group of scientists from Boston University's School of Medicine made some blue mass from a nine-teenth century recipe, and wrote in the journal *Perspectives in Biology and Medicine* that: "Mercury in the form of the blue pill is a potential neurotoxin, which we have demonstrated by recreating and testing the recipe." A neurotoxin is a substance that damages the brain. And while the amount of mercury Lincoln probably consumed was way beyond today's accepted safe level, the scientists add, "Before the main years of his presidency, he was astute enough to recognize the effects and stop the medication soon after his inauguration."

The Medicine Show Era
Before radio, television, or magazines existed, peo-ple learned about manufactured drug products from salesmen who traveled around the country

and talked directly to the public. "Medicine shows" were something like traveling circuses, with enter-tainment to attract the local people, but also featuring enthusiastic salesmen, well trained to convince the public to exchange their dollars for the latest miracle cure. Of course, there were several versions of the most popular products, each claim-ing to be the best. Soon advertising by leaflets and pamphlets was devised as another method to capture the public's interest and money. In fact, some of the earliest printing businesses in the United States were created to print these materials, and then went on to become important newspaper or magazine publishing companies.

Some of the potions and creams of early colonial times boasted of being preferred by European royalty, which made for excellent advertising, just as athletes and celebrities today endorse various products. A king or queen would give permission to the maker of a potion to advertise it as the favorite of the royal house in exchange for a hand-some payment from the maker. In addition, the maker was given official documents called *letters patent* (Latin meaning a document open for the public to read). The *letters patent* gave special rights to the medicine's creator and prohibited other people from making the same product. From that came the phrase "patent medicine," which in the 1800s referred to these specially touted and exclusive products.

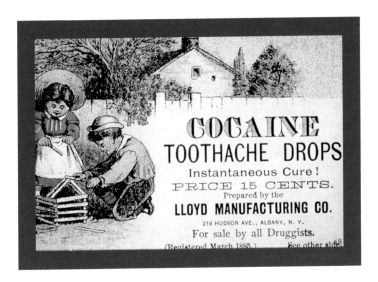

THIS LATE NINETEENTH CENTURY ADVERTISEMENT FOR TOOTHACHE DROPS MADE
WITH COCAINE PROMISED AN "INSTANTANEOUS CURE"—THOSE WHO TOOK THE
DROPS WOULD DEFINITELY FEEL NO PAIN FOR A WHILE.

Patent Medicines Flourish

After the American Revolution severed many rela-
tionships between the colonists and their former
rulers, the opinion of royalty had less clout. "Patent
medicines" came to mean any of the manufactured
concoctions available for purchase. Each had its own
unusual name, such as Hamlin's Wizard Oil, Kick-a-
poo Indian Sagwa, Mug-wump, Dr. Kilmer's Swamp
Root, and Snake Oil Liniment. There were no rules
about what these creations could contain, and
labels didn't have to list ingredients. There even
were radioactive medicines, which weren't known
to be harmful at the time.

Throughout the 1800s, patent medicines could
be created, advertised, and sold without restriction.

IN THE EARLY TWENTIETH CENTURY, THE GOVERNMENT STEPPED IN WITH ITS
"POISON SQUAD" TO DETERMINE WHAT WAS SAFE TO INGEST—AND WHAT WAS
DANGEROUS TO HUMAN HEALTH!

Any sort of healing claim could be made without proof. Some manufacturers even hired people to step out from the audience at medicine shows and say how a product had cured them, when it hadn't.

By the late 1800s, there were enough products being manufactured and sold that a "medicine industry" was flourishing in the United States— an industry without laws, guidelines, or ingredient

The Poison Squad

Dr. Harvey Washington Wiley was determined to make medicines safer for consumers. Beginning in 1883, he was head of the Bureau of Chemistry (something like today's Food and Drug Administration), and he became a tireless leader in getting the Food and Drug Act of 1906 passed. That act was the first to put some restrictions on what medicines could contain and what was written on product labels. He also conducted research on the safety of ingredients in foods and medicines, especially preservatives, using human volunteers. His "Poison Squad," as they were called, captured the fascination (and appreciation) of the nation as they bravely downed such substances as borax, chemical acids, and formaldehyde. The experiments went on for five years. One conclusion Wiley reached was that preservatives such as formaldehyde—which is highly toxic and banned from today's food—should be used only when necessary and listed on the ingredients label, and that the product's manufacturer should have to prove they are safe to consume.

restrictions to protect consumers. That began to change when some courageous and determined citizens started to write about the deception and danger behind these products. A journalist named Samuel Hopkins Adams made a big impact when a series of his articles, called "The Great American Fraud," appeared in the popular magazine *Collier's* in 1905 and 1906.

In an article called "The Subtle Poisons," Adams wrote about several deaths linked to "headache powders"—popular remedies for alleviating headaches, especially among women. Orangeine was one such powder. It didn't have anything from orange fruits in it (it was named for its color and that of its packaging), but did contain a substance (now called acetanilide) which is known today to damage the liver and kidneys, and to interfere with the blood's ability to carry oxygen. Adams described some of the circumstances of the deaths, like this one:

> Last July, an eighteen-year-old Philadelphia girl got a box of Orangeine powders at a drugstore, having been told that they would cure headache. There was nothing on the label or in the printed matter enclosed with the preparation warning her of the dangerous character of the nostrum. Following the printed advice, she took two powders. In three hours she was dead. Coroner Dugan's

verdict follows: "Mary A. Bispels came to her death from kidney and heart disease, aggravated by poisoning by acetanilid taken in Orangeine headache powders."

In warning people about that product, Adams wrote sardonically, "I can conscientiously recommend Orangeine, Koehler's Powders, Royal Pain Powders, and others of that class to women who wish for a complexion of a dead, pasty white, verging to a puffy blueness under the eyes and about the lips."

Adams' articles and other journalists' stories, commentaries, and cartoons exposed the carelessness of the patent manufacturers. The illustrations showed people who had been maimed or killed by poisonous or caustic ingredients. Popular women's magazines such as *Ladies Home Journal* and *Good Housekeeping* were very important in spreading information. In fact, women's groups greatly influenced the final success of getting a law in place to protect consumers from wasting their money on useless and dangerous products.

Government Steps in for Safety
Finally, in 1906, the first governmental regulation went into effect. It was the Food and Drugs Act, also known as the "Pure Food Bill," and it prohibited adding certain harmful ingredients to foods and medicines. There still was no requirement that a

listing of ingredients be printed on a product, but any claim about ingredients had to be truthful—no false claim that snake oil was in a product if it wasn't! Not surprisingly, manufacturers of patent medicines (as well as whiskey producers, who provided the alcohol in many elixirs) had fought strongly against passage of the Food and Drugs Act of 1906. They didn't want the government interfering in sales and profits, or with the "rights" of customers to buy whatever they could be convinced to purchase.

That act certainly didn't stop all the problems. Its restrictions were still much too lax. Some years later, in 1937, a catastrophe got people's attention. A drug called sulfanilamide had been used safely for years in pill or powder form to treat bacterial infections. But a new liquid form, Elixir Sulfanilamide, was made and sold without testing the safety of a new nondrug component: a liquid similar to antifreeze, which is now known to be highly toxic to people and animals. A massive effort was made by the manufacturer and the FDA to warn people and retrieve all the Elixir, once they realized it was killing people. Still, more than a hundred people, mostly children, died because of using that insufficiently tested product.

Dr. A. S. Calhoun wrote at the time, "to realize that six human beings, all of them my patients, one of them my best friend, are dead because they took medicine that I prescribed for them innocently . . . well, that realization has given me such days and nights of mental and spiritual agony as I did not believe a human being could undergo and survive."

Those deaths spurred the passage of the Federal Food, Drug, and Cosmetic Act of 1938, which added many new rules about the manufacture and sale of medicines. Manufacturers had to prove to the federal government—specifically, to the agency known as the Food and Drug Administration (FDA)—that a product was safe before it could be sold to anybody. It also put the federal government in charge of deciding what was safe and what wasn't. Another key provision of the act was that no false claims could be made about health benefits of products. Other rules required safe packaging and labeling, and allowed for government inspections of factories.

In the early 1960s, additional changes were made to the Federal Food, Drug, and Cosmetic Act through Congress-approved amendments. Once again, a tragedy spurred those changes. A popular drug called thalidomide was being used in Europe by thousands of pregnant women to prevent morning sickness (pregnancy-related nausea), until it became clear that the drug was causing terrible birth defects in the children of women who had used the drug. Thousands of children were born with deformed arms or legs that were more like flippers than normal limbs.

Fortunately, thalidomide had not yet been approved in the United States. But the awful story of its impact on a generation of European children was alarming. It was a reminder that there still was too little being done to ensure safety in the increasingly popular pharmaceutical (drug-making) industry. What's more, the drug hadn't really been necessary. Women could have used other, safer products and approaches to minimize their nausea during pregnancy. The realization that thalidomide had caused so much harm and wasn't even necessary led to a new requirement of drug products: that they be really worth using.

A New Era: Proof of Usefulness

The Drug Amendments of 1962 required proof from scientific studies that a drug offered some health benefit. That included products already on the shelves, as well as any new ones. Drug companies were expected to carry out those studies, but they didn't do much to comply. So, in 1966, the FDA finally asked a group of experts from the U.S. National Academy of Sciences to determine as best they could if the products did what their labels and ads claimed they did. The conclusion was shocking: only a fourth of the products were clearly effective, while three-fourths weren't or were open to question.

That disappointing news spurred a larger study sponsored by the FDA. Starting in 1972, seventeen panels of medical experts began to review existing information about the safety and effectiveness of about 700 over-the-counter drugs. Decades of review, discussion, and even court decisions ensued. Finally, in the 1990s, all the panels were finished with their reports. They concluded that a third of over-the-counter ingredients did what their manufacturers claimed, whereas two-thirds either weren't useful, weren't safe, or hadn't been studied well enough to decide.

That was a very disturbing finding for the "modern" age of medicine. It meant, for one thing, that consumers were spending lots of money on products that didn't do what they promised or weren't as safe as they claimed, or both. According to the acts and amendments passed decades earlier, which required safety and effectiveness in OTC drugs, the

BY THE END OF THE TWENTIETH CENTURY, RULES GOVERNING THE PACKAGING AND SALE OF OVER-THE-COUNTER MEDICINES WERE VERY STRICT. HERE, A WORKER INSPECTS DRUGS IN A FACTORY.

majority of OTC products on store shelves were actually illegal because they failed to meet those requirements.

As a result of the panels' reports, more than four hundred ingredients were removed from over-the-counter products. Some of them may have helped, but studies hadn't proven it at the time. Weeding out those products doesn't mean everything on the shelves today really works and is safe for anyone to use. But a great deal of progress has been made toward protecting consumers' health and pocketbooks since the days when medicine shows promised miracles.

3 POPULAR TYPES OF DRUGS SOLD OVER THE COUNTER

Just what are all those over-the-counter products crowding the shelves? Some treat or prevent very common ailments. Examples are pain relievers, allergy medications, cough syrups, anti-itch creams, and bacteria-killing solutions. Other OTC products treat less common ailments or are used only by a specific age group or gender. Laxatives, for example, which encourage movement of food through the intestine, are more familiar to older people because difficulties with digestion are more common among the elderly.

One way to think about all these OTC products is that some treat ailments or illnesses, while others help prevent them. For instance, several kinds of skin lotions help relieve itching caused by bug bites or poison ivy. But there are also products that keep insects away, or remove poison ivy oils thoroughly. Similarly, certain creams treat skin infections, whereas others contain chemicals intended to prevent infection.

A key point about over-the-counter drugs is that they rarely *cure* a problem. Instead, they lessen the symptoms or signs of an ailment. A *symptom* is a physical change in the body that a person feels, like a headache. There are several reasons a person might have a headache, but in many instances a pain reliever will help, whatever the underlying reason. A *sign* refers to a change that other people can observe or measure about a person's body, such as a fever. That, too, can be treated with over-the-counter drugs, but they won't remedy the underlying cause (which usually is an infection).

Still, people want help with tolerating the symptoms and signs while the body's natural healing processes eliminate the underlying problem. And some drug products do cure a problem directly, such as by killing bacteria or fungi that are causing a skin infection.

There are more than eighty categories of OTC drug products. The rest of this chapter will describe the most common OTC categories. A more complete listing of categories, or more detail about those covered here, can be found by consulting the resources listed at the end of this book, or other Internet sites or books written by health care experts.

Pain Relievers and Fever Reducers

Many OTC products offer relief from body aches and pains. People turn to pain relievers (also called analgesics) for problems such as headache, sore throat, discomfort caused by the flu, sports injuries,

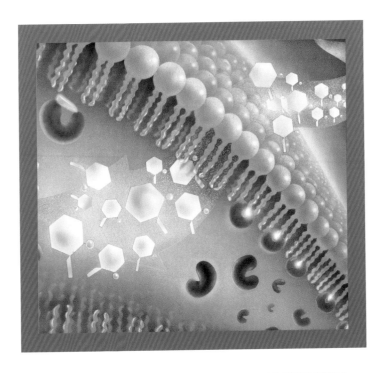

THIS ILLUSTRATION SHOWS HOW ASPIRIN HELPS RELIEVE PAIN BY BLOCKING A CELL'S PRODUCTION OF PAIN-ENHANCING CHEMICALS CALLED PROSTAGLANDINS. AFTER ASPIRIN (BLUE) ENTERS THE CELL'S MEMBRANE (UPPER RIGHT), A PORTION OF ASPIRIN ATTACHES TO AN ENZYME (PURPLE) THAT ORDINARILY WOULD MAKE PROSTAGLANDINS OUT OF SUBSTANCES IN THE CELL'S MEMBRANE (LOWER RIGHT).

toothaches, joint pain, skin injury, menstrual discomfort, and as a transition away from stronger pain relievers that were given after surgery or for a serious injury. Pain relievers come as single drugs or in combinations with other drugs. For example, a very popular combination in cold or allergy remedies is a pain reliever plus a decongestant, which together reduce the discomfort of swollen airways and improve breathing. OTC pain relievers are intended to be taken for a short time—a few days or less. If pain persists longer than that, a doctor should be consulted.

Most OTC pain relievers are NSAIDs, which is short for nonsteroidal anti-inflammatory drugs. The oldest of them is aspirin (acetylsalicylic acid, ASA), originally derived from willow plants, still available and very popular today (also very inexpensive). But there are newer synthetic (made in the laboratory) pain relievers, such as ibuprofen, acetaminophen, and naproxen. Besides relieving discomfort, these synthetic NSAIDs reduce inflammation and fever.

The precise way in which these drugs block the sensation of pain is quite complex and not fully understood. But one important way they do so is by interfering with the production of substances called prostaglandins. Prostaglandins have an array of purposes in the body, and probably contribute to the sensation of pain in several ways. Prostaglandins also enhance inflammation. Inflammation is a reaction to injury or irritation, in which the damaged

Aspirin: An Ancient Drug

Aspirin is a common pain reliever with a centuries-old history. The scientific name of the pain-relieving substance in aspirin is acetylsalicylic acid (ASA for short). Today, ASA is made in the laboratories of drug companies from another chemical, salicin, which is found in plants. (Salicin is actually a plant hormone, with many important roles to play in keeping plants alive and healthy.) But long before chemists discovered salicin, ancient peoples knew that the bark of willow trees, when made into a tea or prepared in other ways, could ease pain and lower fever. Native Americans used white willow bark as a medicinal plant as long ago as the fifth century BCE. In fact, the word salicylic comes from the Latin name for the willow tree (Salix). There are now several other kinds of over-the-counter pain relievers, but aspirin is still extremely popular in many products and forms.

area becomes swollen, tender, reddish, and warm to the touch—all related to an increase in blood flow to the area, which prostaglandins stimulate. The inflammation is reduced, however, if the release of prostaglandins can be lessened. The NSAIDs do just that.

However, NSAIDs also lower the amount of prostaglandins made by cells of the stomach. Those cells, under the stimulation of prostaglandins, normally would be making a layer of moist, slippery mucus, which protects the lining of the stomach and of the upper intestine (into which stomach contents next travel as food is digested) from harsh digestive acid. Without that mucus protection, the stomach or intestinal lining can develop ulcers, which are areas of damaged tissue. Ulcers often bleed and sometimes worsen to become a perforation—a hole that breaks completely through the stomach or intestinal wall. Blood loss because of ulcers or perforation can be bad enough to require emergency blood transfusion, or in some cases, can cause death.

It has long been known that aspirin especially can damage the stomach and cause bleeding. The newer pain relievers have become very popular because they are less irritating to the stomach than aspirin. However, they still cause stomach irritation when taken frequently or at high doses. Scientific studies have discovered that about 15 percent of people who take NSAIDs over a long period develop bleeding. An estimated 10 percent to 50 percent (depending on the study) of people can't tolerate these drugs because of upset stomach or other digestive tract reactions such as diarrhea, bloating, heartburn, or pain. Because of these problems, doctors strongly recommend that NSAIDs only be taken for a few days; their labels carry that warning.

Most pain-relief products are swallowed in pill, capsule, or liquid form. They also come in rub-on (topical) lotions, creams, gels, or sprays, to relieve pain at specific areas of the body, such as an injured muscle or specific joint. Some of the topical products contain NSAIDS or low-dose steroids (more commonly available by prescription). Others contain a skin-numbing ingredient (lidocaine) that interacts with pain-detecting nerves to lessen the pain signals sent by nerves to the brain.

One other way to introduce pain relievers and fever reducers into the body is by suppository. A suppository is a small, gel-like cylinder that is placed into the rectum (the last segment of the intestine). It dissolves at body temperature, releasing its drug into the intestine, where it is absorbed. Suppositories are used for infants and young children and people who are too ill to swallow pills or syrups easily.

Cold, Flu, and Allergy Remedies

The multitude of products created to help with common problems of the airways—colds, flu, and allergies or hay fever—are a reminder that over-the-counter drugs can help us feel better, but don't treat the underlying problem. Colds and influenza are caused by viruses, and OTC products don't destroy viruses (neither do most prescription drugs). The body's immune system must do that. Nevertheless, during the days or weeks the immune system is doing its work, people often choose cold and flu "remedies" to reduce the associated aches and pains, fever, congestion (stuffy nose), and cough.

Airway allergies (hay fever) are the immune system's reaction to inhaled microscopic substances such as pollen or tiny particles of dander (pet hair and saliva). OTC products don't destroy allergens, either. Instead, they tone down the body's reaction to them. Many OTC products do so with an antihistamine drug. Antihistamines work to turn off the effects of the chemical histamine. Histamine is naturally produced by the body, and is an essential chemical player in the process of healing from illness or injury. But too much histamine can make a person miserable. It is released by cells that line the airways when allergens or pathogens (viruses, bacteria) are inhaled. Histamine contributes to a stuffy and runny nose, sneezing, itchy throat, cough—things that are symptoms of allergies as well as a cold or flu.

Cold, flu, and allergy remedies may contain several drugs to treat the many symptoms. These products have different combinations of, for example, a cough suppressant (dextromethorphan), a pain reliever (acetaminophen), and an antihistamine (diphenhydramine). But health experts recommend that, to reduce unnecessary drug intake, people choose a product that will treat only the symptoms that are really bothersome. If a person isn't coughing, a product should be selected that doesn't have the cough suppressant drug. If a person is mostly bothered by a sore throat, a pain reliever could be taken by itself. This approach means carefully reading labels, learning some drug names and their purposes, or consulting with a pharmacist when shopping.

It is also essential to read the labels carefully because some products have different purposes or warnings. The so-called nighttime products have antihistamines that make a person sleepy, so it's important not to use those in the daytime (or even late at night) because the drugs can make a person clumsy, unaware, and slow to react. That makes it very dangerous to drive a vehicle, for example, or use lawnmowers, chainsaws, factory equipment, or other machinery that could cause serious injury.

Digestive Aids
Getting food through the digestive tract isn't always as easy as it should be. Digestion is actually a highly complex activity that is controlled partly by the brain, partly by a network of nerves all along the length of the digestive tract (esophagus, stomach, and small and large intestine), and partly by

ALKA SELTZER IS ONE OF THE MANY OVER-THE-COUNTER MEDICATIONS THAT ACT TO ALLEVIATE HEARTBURN AND INDIGESTION.

hormones that flow between the different regions of the tract. Usually it all works very well, but when something goes awry, a plethora of over-the-counter drug products are there to help.

Some people have a problem with "reflux" of stomach acid, meaning that acid escapes into the lower part of the esophagus (the tube that runs between mouth and stomach), causing pain known as heartburn. The medical term for this problem is GERD—gastroesophageal reflux disease. The most common cause of GERD has to do with the point at which the esophagus connects with the stomach. There, a circle of muscle is meant to temporarily tighten, closing the passage between them while the stomach is secreting acid and digesting food. Acid reflux happens when that closure isn't tight. Many things can weaken the closure, including certain drugs, pregnancy, birth defects, and being overweight.

Antacids are OTC products that neutralize stomach acid, taking the burning sensation away. But they don't address the underlying problem. Moreover, some advertisements for antacids encourage people to continue eating in ways that create heartburn and suggest it is a social duty to do so, in order not to offend the dinner hosts. Certainly that is one way to enjoy a pain-free meal, but such ads encourage people to ignore dealing with the problem in other ways. Also, antacids can generate their own problems, such as constipation or diarrhea, and many contain aluminum, which has been linked to calcium loss from bone.

Another digestive system problem is constipation, or "irregularity," which means difficulty in ridding the digestive tract, through bowel movements, of solid waste (feces, or stool) easily or with normal frequency (each person's frequency of doing so varies, but fewer than three bowel movements a week suggests constipation). Several factors can cause constipation, including emotional upset, certain illnesses, some types of medications, or a change in eating habits. Another cause is too much animal protein or processed foods in the diet and too little "fiber." Fiber refers to plant materials that pass through the digestive tract without being absorbed into the body. Fiber therefore moves down the intestine, adding bulk to the material passing through. That, in turn, stimulates contractions of muscle in the intestinal wall to strongly push things along. Fiber also attracts water, keeping intestinal contents soft and easier to move along.

Over-the-counter aids for constipation are called laxatives or stool softeners. Some are swallowed, while others are suppositories (a solid gel placed in the rectum). Some contain plant fiber that adds bulk; other ingredients attract water; others contain drugs that stimulate contractions of the intestinal muscle; some are combinations of these. And though it can sound harmless to assist with intestinal clearing this way, laxatives can cause harmful reactions with other drugs, and can disturb normal intestinal activity if used too frequently.

The opposite digestive problem is diarrhea. Diarrhea is often caused by infection of the digestive tract with bacteria, viruses, or other organisms. These invaders irritate the intestinal lining, causing inflammation, which triggers frequent contractions of the intestinal muscles. That moves food (and beverage) waste out of the body before much of the fluid can be reclaimed by the large intestine, or bowel. As a result, feces carry a lot of water out of the body.

A person with diarrhea needs to use the toilet frequently, which can interfere with work, school, or other activities. Besides being inconvenient and unpleasant, however, the water loss can change the concentration of important substances in the body and lower blood volume. The condition of having less water in the body than normal is called dehydration, and it can be a real health danger—even deadly. Children are at greater risk than adults of dehydration because their bodies are so small that a small amount of water loss makes a big difference. In fact, diarrhea is one of the main causes of death among children around the world, especially in communities with poor sanitation systems and unclean drinking water. (Those conditions make it easier for digestive tract infections to spread.) By contrast, people who have access to modern waste facilities, clean drinking water, and good medical care rarely die of diarrhea.

Over-the-counter products are very helpful in halting diarrhea. Many contain loperamide, which relaxes intestinal muscles, allowing more water to be absorbed before the waste is pushed out. Bismuth subsalicylate is also a longtime favorite for halting diarrhea. It stops the growth of bacteria that can cause diarrhea and may also reduce fluid loss from cells that line the digestive tract. These drugs also help a person to return to a normal schedule of activities.

Dietary Supplements and Herbal Products

Dietary supplements, herbal products, natural remedies, alternative medicines—all these terms describe a vast collection of plant, mineral, or animal-derived substances that aren't classified as drugs by the U.S. Food and Drug Administration (FDA), but which are readily available as aids for maintaining health and treating ailments. They are sold primarily in natural food stores, but also in other stores alongside OTC products. Many of these herbal products originated in other parts of the world, such as China, India, or South America, where the knowledge of how to make and use them has been passed down for centuries. Other remedies are made from plants that grow in North America, such as *Echinacea* (boosts the immune system), plantain (soothes injured skin and aids healing), and ginseng (enhances energy).

There are hundreds of these products in a wide variety of forms, such as pills, powders, concentrated liquids, teas, pastes, and topical creams. The FDA uses the term "dietary supplement" to refer to those which are taken internally, such as vitamins, minerals, plant materials, amino acids, enzymes, and extracts of animal organs. Dietary supplements are categorized as foods rather than drugs, and the FDA does not require manufacturers to prove the products work or are safe. Instead, manufacturers are expected to ensure product safety and may not make any claims of health benefit unless proven by scientific studies. The FDA does, however, have the authority to stop the sale of products that cause dangerous health effects, and has done so (for example, weight-loss products containing the plant-derived ingredient ephedra). Millions of people use dietary supplements with good results, and there are scientific studies under way to determine the benefits of several promising remedies. But plants contain many potent chemicals, and it is important that someone using a natural remedy do so as recommended by a licensed herbalist, naturopathic doctor, or practitioner of traditional Chinese or Ayurvedic (Indian) medicine, or after consulting a book specializing in the safe usage of herbal products. In addition, some of these products can be dangerous if combined with over-the-counter or prescription drugs, so a doctor or pharmacist should always be consulted before doing so.

Skin Care Products

Many over-the-counter products for the skin are meant to work on the skin's surface. Other products for the skin carry drugs that pass through the skin and penetrate into the bloodstream (such as stick-on patches imbued with nicotine, for people trying to quit smoking). Examples are sunscreens, acne treatments, antiperspirants, bacteria-killing solutions, itch relievers, and medicated soaps.

Sunscreens, or sun block, are possibly the most widely used OTC skin products, at least among Caucasians. These lotions or sprays contain chemicals to absorb ultraviolet (UV) radiation from the sun, thereby preventing such radiation from penetrating the skin. Some amount of sun exposure is fine for most people and helps the body create vitamin D from an inactive precursor molecule, but too much UV exposure has clearly been linked to several forms of skin cancer. (Before that link was recognized, people slathered on suntan oils and lotions instead, which increased the sun's tanning effects on the skin.)

As scientists continue to find decreased amounts of ozone in Earth's upper atmosphere, people with light skin are especially encouraged to use sunscreen during most of their outdoor hours (ozone blocks some UV radiation from reaching Earth). People with dark skin have much larger amounts of the pigment melanin in their skin than do light-skinned people. Melanin is a built-in UV absorber, but sunscreen is nonetheless recommended by skin-care specialists for all but the darkest-skinned people. And the use of protective sunscreens doesn't make it a good idea to spend endless hours basking in the sun. Sunscreens don't block out all wavelengths of UV, and those that do get through are thought to cause faster aging of the skin.

Another type of popular skin care product is acne medication. In the last few decades, a host of soaps, lotions, and creams have been created to reduce the abundance and severity of pimples, which are infections within the pores of the skin. Anti-acne medications contain one or more substances that seem to help by stimulating a natural process of the skin, in which the dead cells on the surface are rubbed off and replaced by new cells deep in the skin. Exactly why this reduces outbreaks of pimples isn't clear. Good antiacne drugs are salicylic acid (similar to, but not the same as aspirin, which is acetylsalicylic acid), resorcinol, sulfur, benzoyl peroxide, and tretinoin. Dermatologists, doctors who specialize in problems of the skin, sometimes recommend using a cream or lotion that kills bacteria as well.

Antiperspirants and deodorants are skin products that deserve mention, too. A deodorant ("remover of odor") is essentially a perfume for the armpits. It isn't intended to reduce sweating. By contrast, an antiperspirant ("against perspiration") contains substances that partly prevent the loss of moisture from the skin, possibly by blocking sweat glands to some degree. Some products are *both* an antiperspirant and deodorant. Antiperspirants can stop some dampness, but they don't seem to work well on the type of sweat glands that get activated by stress and worry—precisely those that eventually can cause odor. It isn't the sweat itself that smells, though. The aroma is due to bacteria that live on the skin and use materials in the sweat as food, and create odoriferous waste products. Deodorants can mask that odor for a while (and bathing can help prevent it). But nothing stops underarm moisture completely. Nor should it—sweating and perspiring are natural body functions.

There are many other types of OTC drug products made to go on the skin: itch relievers, wart removers, athlete's foot and ringworm remedies (both of which kill fungi that grow on the skin), antibacterial liquids and premoistened wipes, "liquid skin" (gluelike liquids that hold cut skin together so it can mend), and many more.

A Wealth of Products
This chapter was a discussion of a small sampling of OTC products. Americans spend huge amounts of money on these drugs to tame the symptoms of some debilitating ailments and illnesses, as well as for minor problems or temporary conditions that would soon go away on their own. Are we too quick to reach for a remedy? One question to ponder before choosing an over-the-counter product is: "Do I really need it, or is advertising convincing me

I do?" Perhaps a change in behavior, such as getting regular exercise, eating more healthfully, or getting more sleep, would make the drug unnecessary.

If the answer is still "Yes, I need help!" then it is important to take some time to read labels carefully, compare products, check warnings, and ask for help from the pharmacist—not just a store clerk—about anything that isn't clear.

- 100% pure BAYER® Aspirin sodium free.
- Starts to work in minutes.

INDICATIONS: Fast acting BAY
recommended for temporary r
and fever of colds, muscle ach
pain, toothache pain, minor a

DIREC
take 1
up to a
directe
unless

**WARNINGS: Children and teer
this medicine for chicken pox
a doctor is consulted about Re
serious illness reported to be**

4 The Safe Use of Over-the-Counter Drugs

Millions of people use over-the-counter products safely, but there are several things to keep in mind when using OTC drugs to be sure they help rather than harm. Precautions begin with three things to check on the package: the information on the label, the expiration date, and the tamper-proof seal.

What's in a Label?
Over-the-counter drug products can be purchased by anyone, at any time, without a doctor's guidance on which product to select and how to use it. That's why information on the product's label is so

important. In fact, one of the FDA requirements about an OTC drug is that instructions about taking it—the who, when, why, and how much—can be written clearly enough on the label for the average person to understand. If those instructions are too complicated, and if misunderstandings could be dangerous, the drug will not be allowed for over-the-counter sale. Instead, using it will require a prescription from a doctor.

These items must be on an OTC label:

- **Product Name:** the name chosen by the manufacturer for the product, which might or might not include the name of its drug ingredient(s) or make it clear what the product is for.

- **Active Ingredient(s):** the substance(s) intended to have a health effect.

- **Inactive Ingredients:** substances in the product that don't have a health effect, but are important for flavor, texture, color, fragrance, and so on.

- **Purpose:** a general category of OTCs to which the product belongs (such as, pain reliever, antihistamine, cough suppressant).

- **Uses:** a description of illnesses or physical problems for which the product is intended.

- **Warnings:** information about possible dangers in using the product, such as side effects that might be experienced while using the product, potentially dangerous interactions when taken with certain other drugs, and what to do in case of an overdose.

Keeping Drugs Secure

Here are some commonsense reminders about keeping drugs away from children, pets, and people wanting to "experiment" with drugs.

- Keep all drug products in high cabinets, preferably ones that can be locked, rather than leaving them on a counter.
- Do not carry pills around in purses, pockets, backpacks, or other easily opened carriers.
- Always keep drugs in a container with a childproof design, and be sure it's closed correctly after each use.
- Never talk about good-tasting medicines or pills as "candy."
- Take medicines privately, so children who may be watching will not mimic your behavior.
- Measure out liquid medicines accurately, using supplied measuring tools or ones purchased from a drugstore. Don't just use any spoon from the silverware drawer. Also, know the difference between tablespoon and teaspoon on label instructions. They are very different sizes!
- Do not allow children, or elderly people with memory problems, to take medicine without supervision.

- **Directions:** instructions on how much to take (or use) of the product and how often. Also states what age groups can take it.
- **Other Information:** tips on storing the product and the amount of certain other ingredients in the product, which are important for some people, such as the amount of calcium, potassium, or sodium.

Deeper into Labeling

Although labels are meant to make it easy for the average person to understand which OTC product to choose and how to use it, it isn't always simple. For instance, labels often are printed in tiny words that can be hard for some people to read while at the store. When in doubt, a shopper can ask a fellow customer, the pharmacist, or a clerk to read the information aloud.

Another problem with labels is that some words aren't familiar to many people. For example, not everyone will know the terms *antitussive* (a drug that lessens the urge to cough) or *expectorant* (a drug that aids in coughing out material that is clogging the lungs and airways). In addition, even simple words can pose a challenge for people whose native language is not the one used on the label.

On the positive side, the FDA takes wording on labels very seriously and updates its rules every now and then about what words can be used. For example, in 1994 it added rules that an OTC product's label could use the word *doctor* instead of *physician*, *ask* instead of *consult*, and *uses* rather than *indications*. And in 1999, the FDA described in a seventy-nine-page document new rules for OTC product labels that would make them easier to read. The rules allowed simpler words, required that the information be listed in a certain order, printed at a certain size or larger, and have a distinctive box surrounding warnings. The FDA's Debra Bowen, who led the effort to improve OTC labels, earned a "No Gobbledygook" award from Al Gore, who was then vice president. (Gore gave such awards in cases in which the federal government helped people understand written information.)

Expiration Date
OTC products don't last forever. With time, drugs break down and lose their strength; well-mixed ingredients separate out; lotions get gummy; fragrances turn unpleasant; adhesives grow old and useless. So it's important to be sure a product isn't too old, especially if it's from a tiny store that may not sell such things too often, and has had a supply on the shelf collecting dust for months or years.

Somewhere on an OTC product there should be an expiration date. This date indicates when the manufacturer believes the product will be too old to be reliable. Most stores remove products from the shelves when they get past their expiration dates, though not every store keeps up with that task, and some even put expired products on sale to get rid of

Checklist for Safe Use of Over-the-Counter Products

- Do some research about an over-the-counter drug *before* taking it.
- Read the label on the product thoroughly and in good light. Check if the label is folded, with more information inside or on the back.
- Make no assumptions about a product: check its ingredients and dosage each time you purchase it.
- Always heed dosages, age restrictions, and warnings on the product label.
- Select a product with the least number of drugs necessary to treat symptoms; avoid products with drugs that aren't needed.
- Don't take over-the-counter drugs and prescription drugs for the same condition at the same time.
- Keep an up-to-date list of the names and doses of all drugs you are taking and carry a copy in your wallet or purse.
- Consult a doctor or pharmacist before taking any over-the-counter drug while taking any prescription medications.

- Never take a drug offered by someone else unless you are certain what the drug is and how to use it safely.
- Be sure tamper-proof seals are intact before purchase and first usage.
- Be sure the expiration date on a product has not passed.
- Keep drug products out of the reach of children and pets.
- Make sure childproof containers are closed properly.
- Never allow children to measure out their own medicines.
- Never give adult medicines to children.

them. It falls to the consumer to check that the expiration date hasn't passed when buying a product. In fact, the date should be some months (or years) ahead of the current date. It's no use buying a bottle with enough pain reliever for a year if it expires in a week.

It is also important to check the expiration date of something that has been in the household a while. Its useful life may have come and gone while in the medicine cabinet. When getting a new version at the store, check ingredient listings and dosage because manufacturers sometimes change a product while keeping the old (or similar) packaging and product name.

Tamper-Proof Packaging
Sadly, a few individuals over the years have committed criminal acts by secretly adding injurious ingredients to OTC products and harming people who used those products. To prevent this from happening again, products now have special tamper-evident (also called tamper-proof) features, which seal the lids or packages at the factory, under close supervision, and which become broken only when the item is opened by a consumer. One example is a plastic screw cap attached to a plastic ring around the neck of the bottle or jar. The cap breaks off the ring when it is twisted. Another is a clear plastic layer tightly enclosing the entire product. It is a criminal offense for anyone except the person who buys the product to alter tamper-proof packaging.

Here's how to make sure products haven't been tampered with:

- Inspect the product to find its tamper-proof seal (it may be explained on the package).
- Don't buy anything that appears damaged, loose, or open.
- Don't use a product that looks discolored or odd. When in doubt, return it to the store or show it to a pharmacist.
- Never use a product that isn't sealed unless you know where it's been, or know and trust the person who is giving it to you!

Keeping Kids Safe

Some of the products on drugstore shelves are made especially for children. There are many reasons for this. Often those products are flavored or chewable (instead of needing to be swallowed whole). Many are colorful and "cute," and therefore more interesting to kids. But most importantly, children's medicines typically contain less of an OTC drug per dose than do adult versions because a child's body is smaller. Also, a child's metabolism is slower, so it can take days for a child's body to clear the same dose of a drug that an adult's body clears in a few hours.

In some cases, OTC products don't come in a children's version, but an adult's product describes the dosage that is right for children. This is only allowed by the FDA if scientific studies have determined how much is safe for children, and at what age. Often there is an age below which the drug's

OVER-THE-COUNTER MEDICINES NOW HAVE CAPS THAT ARE TRICKY TO PULL OFF, SO THAT A CHILD COULD NOT ACCIDENTALLY SWALLOW LOTS OF PILLS OR CAPSULES.

safety hasn't been studied, and that age limit will be clearly stated on the label. A drug must never be given to a child younger than the specified age limit.

Virtually all drug products come in childproof containers. Some of these containers require a very strong grip or pressure, which keeps out children but also makes it difficult for some adults with injuries or disabilities to get them open. For that reason, drug manufacturers are allowed to sell one version of their product in a container that anyone can open. It's important to choose that product only if children are not in the home, and to keep it out of reach when children visit.

Safety for Baby
Another important way to keep children safe from the harm that can result from over-the-counter drug usage is to begin when they are still in a mother's

protective womb. Many substances pass from the mother's bloodstream into the fetus, including OTC and prescription drugs. Doctors and researchers believe that at least 10 percent of birth defects are caused by substances in the mother's bloodstream, such as medications, supplements, cleaners, and pesticides. And while very few studies have been done on the effects of OTC or prescription drugs on human fetuses (it would be unethical to expose pregnant women to drugs intentionally for testing purposes), studies using animals show the potential for several drugs—including a few common OTC products—to cause fetal abnormalities. Doctors recommend, for example, that the common pain-relievers—aspirin, ibuprofen (Advil, Motrin), and naproxen (Aleve)—be avoided during pregnancy because they may be associated with several serious fetal defects (acetaminophen is considered safest).

Alcohol is another example of a drug known to cause birth defects. Alcohol is present in some common OTC cold and allergy medications, and though the overall amount isn't very great per dose, the U.S. Centers for Disease Control and Prevention assert that any amount of alcohol may put the fetus at risk of brain damage, physical deformities, and other irreversible abnormalities.

The bottom line for a pregnant woman is: Always read warnings on labels. Any OTC (or prescription) drug that is suspected of causing harm to the fetus carries a warning on its label. Also, pregnant women should consult a doctor or pharmacist before taking *any* over-the-counter product because new information may be available that is not on the label. The same holds for women who are breast-feeding a baby because many drugs in the mother's body get into breast milk.

Governmental Watchdog: FDA

Since the beginning of the twentieth century, the federal government has played a role in watching over the safety of drug products and in keeping companies honest in their claims about what the products do. The part of government that is responsible for doing so is the Food and Drug Administration (FDA), and within it, the Center for Drug Evaluation and Research (CDER).

When the FDA was formed, many drugs already were being used. In addition, new ones were being invented or discovered by the drug companies. One huge task CDER had was to decide about drugs that were already being used. Which ones were truly safe and useful? Which were causing too many bad side effects? Could harmful ones be made safe by putting better instructions on the label? CDER has done its research on many of those drugs and decided which qualify as good over-the-counter substances, and which must be discontinued (or shifted to a prescription-only category).

CDER's other task is ongoing: to review requests from drug companies to allow new drugs onto the market. That process usually takes years because many studies must be done on new drugs—first on

Healing Wisdom from Around the World

The healing wisdom of cultures around the globe has captured the interest of many people in the United States, including some mainstream doctors. Descriptions of ancient healing traditions like Chinese or Ayurvedic (Indian) medicine, which are still widely practiced today, are available in numerous books, magazines, Internet sites, classes, and from "natural medicine" experts including herbalists, naturopathic doctors, and specialists in Chinese or Ayurvedic medicine. Some scientists and researchers (including representatives of drug companies) are traveling the world to learn about folk remedies from indigenous people who live much as they always did, without a drugstore or pharmacist anywhere in sight. These cultures, like some rainforest-dwelling tribes in South America, typically have a wise elder, such as a shaman, "medicine man" (or woman), or *curandera*, who is especially revered for his or her knowledge of how to use wild plants as medicines. Some are willing to share their secrets with others outside the tribe, some are not. Understandably, they are protective of their land and their culture, and don't want to be exploited.

animals, then on a small group of people to check that the drug is safe, then on many more people to check safety again and to see if the drug really does something useful. If the drug appears to be safe (for most people) and useful, CDER will approve it for sale to the public, either as an OTC or prescription product.

It's important to realize that CDER does not do its own research about the safety and usefulness of new drugs. Instead, the companies that make the drugs do the studies. (Usually companies collaborate with doctors at hospitals and medical schools because that's where people with ailments and illnesses are easy to find.) When the studies are completed, the drug companies give their results to CDER, which decides whether or not to approve the drug.

It may sound a little odd that companies that want to sell their products are also in charge of collecting the data that prove how safe and useful they are. It is sort of like asking a student to write and grade her own test and then show the teacher how it went. Some people question whether the studies are really trustworthy. In fact, there recently has been quite a stir among consumers and many medical professionals who want the Food and Drug Administration to require drug manufacturers to show all data from their studies (not just the data that show a drug in a good light). The FDA is considering doing so.

What's more, in 2004 a group of eleven prominent medical journals, which publish the results of drug studies, said they would no longer print results if only the drug company had access to the data. Some drug companies have voluntarily set up Web sites to make their data public. But, as Catherine De Angelis, editor-in-chief of the *Journal of the American Medical Association*, points out, that may not be enough to keep drug companies honest about how safe and effective their drugs appear from those studies. "Why would you put the fox in charge of the hen house?" she asks. The companies could just leave data they didn't like off the Web pages.

Wouldn't it be better if someone else did the studies—someone who had no preference about the outcome? The problem is that the FDA and CDER do not have enough money or employees to do all the work that would be needed. Drug manufacturers, with billions of dollars of income each year, are the only ones who can afford the studies.

There are other problems with this drug-approval system. Consumer safety groups sometimes accuse the FDA of approving a new drug when medical experts strongly recommend holding back on approval until more studies are done. But doctors and people with illnesses also accuse the FDA of delaying approval of a new drug that might be a patient's only hope.

Clearly, the system that tests drug safety is not perfect. As a consumer, it's your job to do some research about a drug before taking it.

ADVERTISING CAN PLAY A PIVOTAL ROLE IN OUR USE OF OVER-THE-COUNTER MEDICATIONS. DO WE REALLY NEED TO KEEP OUR ARMPITS DRY AT ALL TIMES? A TRIP TO THE SUPERMARKET WOULD TELL US SO, BUT SWEATING IS A NATURAL PHENOMENON.

5 CONCERNS ABOUT OVER-THE-COUNTER DRUGS

Labels on OTC products describe how to use them safely, and most people will have no problems as long as those instructions are heeded. Nevertheless, it is important to understand that there are health risks in using OTC products. Some risks are in the consumer's control, but others are not, such as unforeseen problems that can arise when a person uses a drug for many years—longer than studies of the drug's safety lasted. Allergies or other unpleasant or harmful reactions to the drug, or to inactive ingredients, may also occur.

Yet another problem is societal. The sheer quantity of drug products, and their persuasive advertisements, are changing the way we think about our health and bodies. People are losing trust in the body's natural healing abilities. Some feel helpless and fearful about dealing with ailments without the aid of a drug product. Advertising is even changing what people think about how the human body should look, feel, and smell.

These and other concerns about OTC products are the focus of this chapter. Many of these concerns also apply to prescription drugs, but doctors determine who will take those. OTC products, by contrast, are available to anybody at any time, in any amount.

People Make Mistakes

One of the greatest drawbacks of over-the-counter products is that people occasionally use them without fully reading the instructions and warnings on the label. Sometimes it just doesn't seem necessary. Who would suspect that a person with diabetes or poor circulation shouldn't use wart remover? Yet the chemical in wart removers (salicylic acid) digests skin cells, which requires healing, and healing is often slow in people with poor circulation or diabetes. A serious skin infection could result if bacteria settle in before the area has healed over.

Or a parent might choose a stomach-soothing OTC liquid to ease the upset stomach of a child or teenager with a viral infection, such as chicken pox or flu. But there is evidence that during a viral infection the salicylate chemical in some of these products increases the likelihood that young people will get Reye's syndrome, a rare illness that damages many organs and sometimes kills. For that reason, aspirin and any other products containing salicylates (a group of related drugs) should be avoided during a viral infection. Fortunately, these products carry warnings on the label.

And people still make mistakes. Someone might use a cold remedy he or she has often used before, but forget that it contains the kind of antihistamine that causes drowsiness. That person may then get in the car and drive, without realizing the drug was diminishing the brain's ability to make quick decisions and the muscles' ability to act. The result could be a car crash with serious injuries or fatalities. Such things really happen.

But most people agree that human errors aren't enough of a reason to keep OTC products off the shelf. So it is up to each person to follow all directions and heed all warnings.

Adverse Reactions
All drugs will, upon occasion, cause reactions in some people that have nothing to do with the ailment for which a person would take the drug. These reactions are called side effects. When the side effects are unpleasant or harmful, they are called adverse reactions or adverse events. (Note, however, that *side effects* often is used interchangeably with *adverse reactions* to mean only undesirable drug effects.) Adverse reactions can be minor, such as a

slight headache, a bit of intestinal gas, nausea, or a skin rash. But other reactions, such as a severe allergic reaction or intestinal bleeding, can be life-threatening.

What consumers often don't realize is that virtually all studies that "prove" a drug to be safe also find adverse reactions. But that doesn't necessarily prevent the drug from getting approved and being sold to the public. Governmental approval of a drug is a balancing game that weighs a drug's benefits against its problems. The U.S. Center for Drug Evaluation and Research (part of the FDA) explains to consumers in its educational materials that some problems may not show up until after a drug has been approved and used by many people. Drugs that are considered safe enough for OTC sales aren't required to mention any adverse reactions on the label. Some drugs are deemed beneficial but too dangerous for the OTC market, and are sold by prescription only, in which case the adverse reactions must be listed.

NSAIDs (nonsteroidal anti-inflammatory drugs, such as aspirin and ibuprofen) exemplify a balance between benefit and adverse reactions. NSAIDs are among the most widely used OTC drugs. They relieve pain, reduce inflammation, and lower fever. They are common ingredients of remedies that reduce symptoms of colds, allergies, and flu. But NSAIDs can cause digestive tract irritation, which may appear as nausea, cramps, heartburn, constipation, or diarrhea. They can also cause digestive tract bleeding and ulceration (irritation and cell damage to the stomach or intestine). Bleeding often goes unnoticed and leads to a gradual reduction in a person's blood volume. That can cause anemia, a condition of having too little blood to deliver enough oxygen to the body. A person with anemia can experience dizziness, extreme tiredness, headaches, and even loss of consciousness. Sometimes NSAIDs taken for months or years cause enough blood loss to endanger a person's life due to heart failure or serious damage to blood-deprived organs. That can happen suddenly, when an ulcerated area breaks open and blood vessels leak a lot of blood at once.

NSAIDs are an example of how adverse reactions might only become apparent after a product has been used by thousands or millions of people for several years. Another example concerns the many antacids and antiperspirants that contain aluminum. Using them increases the amount of aluminum in the body, which normally is very low. Scientific studies report that high aluminum levels appear to cause calcium bone loss, which may lead to osteoporosis (a condition of having abnormally fragile bones). Another concern about aluminum is that it is present in abnormally high amounts in the brains of people who died of Alzheimer's disease. It isn't yet clear whether that aluminum might have accumulated there over years and *caused* Alzheimer's disease, or is just a consequence of it. But many health experts encourage people to avoid taking in aluminum, whether in the form of antacids, aluminum-containing antiperspirants, or foods cooked in aluminum pots or stored in aluminum cans or wrappings.

It would be helpful to consumers to know what problems people are having with OTC drugs. Unfortunately, CDER does not require anybody to report adverse reactions to them about OTC products, though consumers can write or call CDER voluntarily. But CDER has no set plan of what to do with such information.

Fortunately, the Internet has become a powerful sounding board and information-sharing hub. Consumers, doctors, and other medical experts have created Web sites to post problems and warnings as they experience adverse reactions to drugs. People without Internet access at home can visit a public library to use computers and get assistance in searching for such information. In addition, books such as *The People's Pharmacy*, by Joe and Teresa Graedon, inform consumers of problems associated with some OTC (and prescription) drugs.

Allergic Reactions

Some people know they are allergic to a certain drug, so they avoid taking that drug and anything chemically similar to it. They know they need to read the labels of OTC products carefully because drugs often show up on ingredients lists where they might not be expected. People also can be allergic to the nondrug ingredients in a product—the dyes, flavorings, fragrances, thickeners, and so on. These people must use products without the item that triggers the allergy (if they know what it is). Such products can be hard to find.

Some allergic reactions may simply be a nuisance, causing itchy skin or a scratchy throat, but other reactions can be severe and require emergency medical care. Breathing can become difficult as airways suddenly narrow. Blood volume can drop sharply as water from the bloodstream leaks out of blood vessels into tissues. Without receiving enough blood, the brain malfunctions and can trigger seizures or unconsciousness. These changes can actually be fatal.

Drug labels warn consumers not to use a product if they already know they are allergic to an ingredient. But the only way a person can know that is by having had, at some earlier time, an allergic reaction to it. That doesn't help people who haven't yet tried the product. Before using a drug product for the first time, it's a good idea to ask the pharmacist if allergic reactions are a known problem with that product and what kinds of symptoms or signs to watch for. Also, it's a good idea to only use a new drug product when emergency medical help would be available. Trying out that new cold remedy while out in the wilderness somewhere isn't a great idea if it ends up triggering a severe allergic response.

Leaving People Out

Another problem with OTC products is that testing for safety doesn't include everyone. Safety studies are done with specially selected groups of volunteers who often are young to middle-aged Caucasian men. But if a drug is proven safe for them, that doesn't mean it will be safe for women, the elderly, or other races (and differences among these groups in how drugs work definitely exist). Longer studies include more women, but rarely a better racial mix (and pregnant women are usually not included in studies).

Some studies of drug safety require volunteers to be perfectly healthy. Other studies use volunteers who have the ailment for which the drug is being tested (such as a cold), but will not use volunteers who have other health problems, such as liver or kidney disease, or who are using other drugs. But once the product is approved and put on the market, anyone can use it, including people with health conditions that might make the drug product dangerous, or who are taking other drugs, vitamins, or other substances whose combined effects (with the drug product) were not tested.

If a person has liver disease, for instance, or consumes a lot of alcohol (which damages liver cells), many drugs will have longer-lasting effects in that person. That's because a damaged liver can't do one of its most important tasks: break down substances in the bloodstream that aren't natural to the body—

like drugs. The liver's ability to break down drugs into inactive substances is the reason a drug's effects eventually wear off. If the liver is unhealthy, drugs remain in the bloodstream for a longer time and accumulate with each additional dose. That can cause a dangerous overdose. And while an OTC label may warn people with liver disease to avoid the product, some people may not realize they have liver problems.

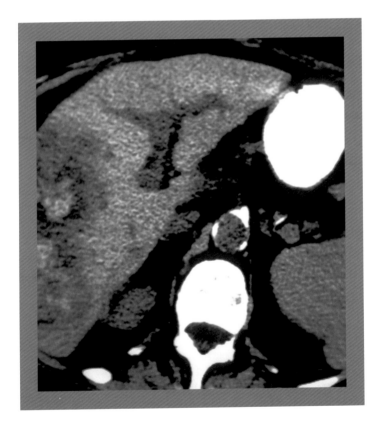

ONE OF THE MOST COMMON PAIN RELIEVERS—ACETAMINOPHEN—HAS BEEN SHOWN TO SERIOUSLY DAMAGE THE LIVER IN SOME CASES.

Several studies have found that one of the most common pain-relievers, acetaminophen, can seriously damage the liver in some circumstances. A five-year study from 1998 to 2003 found that 275 people across the nation who suffered acute liver failure (severe damage to the liver so it cannot function) had been consuming high doses of acetaminophen, often in combination with alcohol. Because of these studies, the American Liver Foundation, the nation's leading nonprofit organization promoting liver health, warns that people "who regularly consume three or more alcoholic beverages daily should take no more than two grams per day of acetaminophen without consulting their physician." A similar warning is now printed on many, but not all, products containing acetaminophen. Researchers are collecting data to decide if the other NSAID pain-relievers can damage the liver.

Additional testing on children is required before a product can be advertised as safe for children. Children's bodies have slower drug-clearing abilities than healthy adults, which is why adult medicines should never be given to children unless the label says children can take the drug.

Are Inactive Ingredients Really Inactive?
It seems odd that many toothpastes and mouthwashes warn the user not to swallow them. What's in those products that we shouldn't be swallowing?

(And doesn't that always happen a little bit when a liquid is swirled around in the mouth for a few minutes?) Besides, many substances are easily absorbed into the body across the lining of the mouth.

One of the ingredients of concern in these products is fluoride, added in small amounts to strengthen teeth. But it can also permanently discolor children's teeth, and is toxic if taken internally. The FDA knows that swallowing fluoride-containing toothpaste or mouth rinses can poison children, so it requires this warning to be printed on the tubes: "Keep out of the reach of children under 6 years of age. In case of accidental ingestion, seek professional assistance or contact a Poison Control Center immediately."

Toothpaste and mouthwashes also have artificial sweeteners, such as saccharin, aspartame, and acesulfame. These are added to improve the flavor of the paste or liquid, and they don't promote cavities because cavity-causing bacteria can't use them for food, as they can with regular sugar. And although these artificial sweeteners were approved by the FDA as safe in food products, there is a troubling amount of evidence that they can cause brain disorders and a host of other harmful reactions in some people. Several physicians and other health specialists have voiced their worries about these substances and have written books, given lectures, hosted Web sites, and talked with government officials about the dangers of these "inactive" ingredients.

The artificial dyes and preservatives in OTC products also are a concern because studies using animals, and some with people, implicate these substances as carcinogens or disrupters of normal hormonal functioning. The Internet and many bookstores provide information that isn't included on product labels. And why not look for a drug product with the least number of nondrug substances? Anything listed as an inactive ingredient is optional as far as the drug's effect, except in a very few cases (as with certain pills that release their drug content slowly over time, in which case the material around the drug is important).

Drug Interactions

With so many different kinds of medications available today, from prescription and over-the-counter drugs to herbal products and vitamin supplements, there is a danger that someone may take some of these in a combination that creates adverse reactions. Many OTC drugs are known to interact with other substances in a person's bloodstream, especially prescription drugs. Because of these interactions, prescription drugs come with warnings about what other substances must be avoided while taking the drug. Consumers must remember that OTC products might be included in these warnings. And if a doctor who is about to prescribe a drug asks what other drugs a patient is taking, that means OTC (and vitamin and herbal) products as well as prescription drugs.

One commonsense rule when taking any drug product (OTC or prescription) is to avoid combining things that have the same effect on the body. For instance, alcohol has a sedative effect on the brain, causing (among other things) a slowing of heart rate and of breathing. Some prescription drugs, such as sleeping pills and antianxiety medicines, are sedatives. Some OTC drugs are sedatives, too, such as the antihistamines found in dozens of OTC products. Alcohol is present in many cold and cough remedies. Combining any of these sedatives is very risky. Doing so can slow the heart and breathing rate to dangerously low levels.

Other dangerous drug interactions would be hard to predict, and have been discovered only as more and more people use a drug. For example, aspirin interacts with dozens of other drugs, including a very popular prescription drug (enalapril) that can protect certain people with high blood pressure or heart disease from dying. But aspirin can counteract enalapril's effects, making it useless. Anyone who doesn't know about that drug interaction and takes them both might die.

Many other OTC drugs interact with substances that might be in a person's bloodstream. It is essential to read a label for warnings about these possibilities, and to check with a pharmacist, doctor, or reputable medical Web sites, such as those posted by the FDA, drug manufacturers, and medical experts, for the latest information about drug interactions.

Overdose

As with prescription drugs, OTC drugs can be dangerous if a person takes an overdose. Labels tell consumers how much to take and how often, but overdoses still happen. Perhaps a child finds some pills that were left open, or enjoys a drink from a fruit-flavored, drug-rich elixir. An elderly person might forget having already taken a dose and repeat it. Or an error might be made when reading the label.

Overdosing on OTC products can require emergency medical attention. To get the point across, here is a collection of overdose symptoms for those very popular cold/cough/allergy medications: cold, clammy skin; extreme confusion; hallucinations; convulsions (seizures); severe drowsiness or dizziness; extreme nervousness or restlessness; fixed pinpoint pupils of eyes; fast, pounding, or slow heartbeat; unusually slow, fast, or troubled breathing; severe weakness; diarrhea; nausea or vomiting; stomach cramps or pain; swelling or tenderness in the upper abdomen or stomach area; loss of hearing; vision problems; intense thirst; uncontrollable flapping movements of the hands (especially in elderly patients).

Remember: OTC drugs are not necessarily harmless. Keeping them safely locked away and properly closed in childproof containers will help prevent accidental overdose. Pill containers with compartments for each day of the week can help forgetful people—or those who take a lot of pills—to keep track of their daily dose.

Dependence on OTC Drugs

One of the definitions of OTC drugs is that they don't create dependence—a physical or psychological need for the drug. Some contain drugs such as codeine that are known to create physical dependence at higher doses, but in small amounts aren't meant to get people hooked.

Some people, however, report feeling addicted to OTC products. Nasal decongestants (drops or sprays) are among them. In *The People's Pharmacy*, authors Joe and Teresa Graedon mention several people who described a habit they couldn't kick of using nasal decongestant spray daily, often several times, and doing so for years, though the products are meant to be used for a few days. Similarly, some people have trouble stopping pain medication (many of which contain caffeine in addition to the painkiller), or enjoy just a little too much the sedative effect of a nighttime cold remedy, with its alcohol and antihistamine.

Some of the dependence being reported could be psychological, related to the soothing familiarity of repeating a behavior, or the confidence that a product is doing some good. But the long-term potential for OTC dependence seems real and deserves study. So far, it may be that dependence problems arise only when OTC products are used for too long, in too high a dose, or too often. Each of these behaviors can increase the level of active ingredients in the bloodstream above what was deemed safe when the product was approved for over-the-counter sale. Dextromethorphan (DXM), a narcotic derivative included in more than a hundred over-the-counter medications, has become a drug of abuse called Triple C, Skittles, and Red Devils (for the color of the pills). Taken in large overdose (ten times or more than the recommended dose), dextromethorphan creates hallucinations. But it can cause a loss of muscle control, unconsciousness, and death. It also causes dependence.

Sweeping Symptoms under the Rug

One of the main concerns about the use of over-the-counter products is that people are trying to "fix" something themselves without medical training. Of course, many ailments can be treated without a doctor's credentials, but when drugs diminish symptoms, they can keep a person from seeking help for the underlying cause. For example, recurrent backache might be due to poor posture while spending hours at the computer. Taking pain relievers can eliminate the pain, but the backache can serve as a helpful reminder to get up often and stretch, or get some exercise (and maybe a new chair)—which would be better for long-term back health. Or something much more serious might be wrong with the person's backbone or nerves, which should be treated by a doctor.

Or perhaps someone is taking a painkiller to treat a sore throat, thinking it is a symptom of a simple cold or flu, only to find out when it doesn't get better that it's "strep throat," a serious bacterial infection that can spread to the heart, brain, and other organs with very damaging results. A visit to the doctor sooner and some prescription antibiotics could have eliminated the infection early on.

And although OTC products help a sick person feel better, health experts caution that some of the symptoms of illness are important to getting well, and that dampening them may actually prolong the illness. For instance, an excess of mucus (the sticky material that clogs the airways during a cold, flu, or allergy) helps capture viruses, bacteria, pollen, or other irritating substances, and coughing is the body's way of clearing out pathogen-laden mucus. Drugs that turn off the body's impulses to cough get in the way of an important natural method of cleaning up the airways. On the other hand, if bouts of coughing are keeping a person awake through the night, a cough suppressant can provide some hours of sound sleep, which also aids in the healing process.

Problems, or Persuasive Ads?

A final concern about some over-the-counter products is that they create the impression that we need to fix things that are just part of being human. Some suggest, for example, that it's not right to have damp areas in the armpits of clothing, and yet

Drug, or Cosmetic?

Many products on store shelves are easy to think of as drugs, such as cough syrups and pain relievers. But what about products such as antiperspirants, face creams, sunblocking makeup, and antidandruff shampoos? Those are usually thought of as cosmetics or "personal care products," but may also contain drugs. In the United States, the FDA (Food and Drug Administration) decides whether a product is a drug or a cosmetic, based on definitions in the Federal Food, Drug, and Cosmetic Act of 1938. That act says it depends on the intended use, and defines a drug as something intended for "the diagnosis, cure, mitigation, treatment, or prevention of disease" and which are "intended to affect the structure or any function of the body of man or other animals." (Note that when the act was written, it was understood that "man" meant men, women, and children.) By contrast, cosmetics are "for cleansing, beautifying, promoting attractiveness, or altering appearance." Obviously, many products nowadays are both drugs and cosmetics, such as toothpastes that contain fluoride, and deodorants (which are fragrances) that are also antiperspirants (which prevent perspiration). Such products must meet all the regulations about safety and advertising for both cosmetics and drugs.

sweating is a natural part of human physiology. Other ads tell us the fresh aroma of mint on the breath is needed to prevent a dating disaster. We are told that as we age, it must not show: men must use hair-growth products to look younger than they are, and women are convinced by advertisements that they have numerous age-related "problems" for which they need to take drug products.

Other advertising tells us we must make sterile environments of our mouths and skin by using mouthwashes and cleansers to kill bacteria, even though the body has its own natural defenses, such as bacteria-killing enzymes in saliva and acidic secretions on the skin. Women are encouraged to cleanse their vaginas, ignoring the fact that doing so removes naturally occurring secretions that help keep that area free of disease.

Even schoolchildren learning about "the birds and the bees" are given advertising packets and product samples, attempting to convince them they'll be outcasts if they sweat or smell, and that it's a sign of being a grownup to use the latest OTC products. There are many more examples of the way drug manufacturing companies are redefining what it means to be a healthy human being. These companies are making billions of dollars by convincing the public it takes the use of their products for a person to be healthy and happy.

Of course, many OTC products really help with nagging symptoms of illness, and cause little or no obvious problems. Many make our ailments tolerable and allow us to carry on busy lifestyles in relative comfort. The choice to use them, and to do so properly and safely, is literally in the consumer's hands.

GLOSSARY

addictive—A characteristic of a substance or behavior in which a person develops a powerful physical or psychological need for that substance or behavior. *See also* **dependence**.

adverse reaction—An undesirable side effect of a drug. Some are minor (headache, skin rash), while others can be life-threatening (seizures, bleeding).

analgesic—A pain reliever.

antihistamine—A popular category of OTC drugs that reduces inflammation, relieving symptoms of hay fever, colds, and flu.

brand—A company's name and logo, which gets printed on its products. Consumers have many OTC brands to choose from when selecting a product at the store.

CDER—Center for Drug Evaluation and Research, a subdivision of the U.S. FDA (Food and Drug Administration), which is responsible for regulating the safety and effectiveness of drug products.

dependence—Having a physical or psychological need for a substance. (Dependence increasingly is replacing the word addiction.)

generic—A drug that is manufactured by a company other than the original inventor of it, which is possible legally only after the inventor's patent has expired (usually twenty years).

inactive ingredient(s)—Substance(s) in a product that don't have a health effect, but are important for its flavor, texture, color, fragrance, etc.

inflammation—A reaction by the body to injury or irritation that causes swelling, redness, pain, and warmth at the site. It is a natural beginning of the healing process, but if excessive, can actually injure organs, block airways, cause brain swelling, and more.

NSAIDS—Abbreviation for nonsteroidal anti-inflammatory drugs, which are common pain relievers that work (in part) by blocking the body's production of prostaglandins. These are different from steroidal anti-inflammatory drugs (made of steroid molecules), which are usually sold by prescription and work differently.

pharmaceutical company—A company that makes over-the-counter and prescription drugs and drug products; drug-manufacturing company.

side effect—A reaction a person has to a drug that is not part of its intended effect. Those that are undesirable are called adverse reactions or adverse events, although the term "side effects" is often used to mean only undesirable reactions.

sign—A change in the body, due to illness or a health problem, which can be measured, such as quickened heart rate or fever.

symptom—A change in the body, due to illness or a health problem, that a person feels but which cannot be easily measured, such as a headache.

topical—For use on the skin.

FURTHER INFORMATION

Books

Garrison, Robert. *Pharmacist's Guide to Over-the-Counter Drugs and Natural Remedies: A Guide to Finding Quick and Safe Relief*. Garden City Park, NY: Avery, 1999.

Graedon, Joe, and Teresa Graedon. *The People's Pharmacy*. New York: St. Martin's Press, 1998.

Griffith, H. Winter, and Stephen W. Moore. *Complete Guide To Prescription and Nonprescription Drugs*. NY: Perigree Trade Books, 2005.

Monroe, Judy. *Herbal Drug Dangers*. Berkeley Heights, NJ: Enslow Publishers, 2000.

Reader's Digest Guide to Over-The-Counter Drugs. Reader's Digest Association, 2002.

White, Linda, and Steven Foster. *The Herbal Drugstore: The Best Natural Alternatives to Over-the-Counter and Prescription Medicines!* Rodale Books, 2001.

Web Sites

Center for Drug Evaluation and Research (CDER): The agency within the Food and Drug Administration that oversees drug safety and development. http://www.fda.gov/cder/Offices/OTC/consumer.htm

The Health Research Group: A nonprofit group promoting safer drugs and citizen education, and advocating for legislation to protect consumers. http://www.citizen.org/hrg

MedlinePlus: Information about prescription and over-the-counter drugs (sponsored by the National Library of Medicine and the National Institutes of Health). http://www.nlm.nih.gov/medlineplus/druginformation.html

National Institute on Drug Abuse for Teens http://www.teens.drugabuse.gov

PDR® Family Guide to Over-The-Counter Drugs: Online database of information about over-the-counter drugs. http://www.gettingwell.com/drug_info/otcdrugprofiles/alphaindexa.shtml

BIBLIOGRAPHY

Adams, Samuel Hopkins. "The Subtle Poisons" *Collier's*: December 2, 1905.

American Liver Foundation. "Position Statement on Acetaminophen Use and Liver Injury." http://www.liverfoundation.org/db/advocacy/1001 (Accessed February 9, 2006)

"Antacids." *The Merck Manual of Medical Information, Online Version.* http://www. merck.com/mmhe/sec02/ch018/ch018g.html (Accessed February 9, 2006)

Ballentine, Carol. "Taste of Raspberries, Taste of Death: The 1937 Elixir Sulfanilamide Incident." *FDA Consumer* (June 1981). http://www.fda.gov/oc/history/elixir.html (Accessed January 29, 2006)

Black, Ronald A., and D. A. Hill. "Over-the-Counter Medications in Pregnancy". *American Family Physician* 67, no. 12 (June 15, 2003): 2517–2524. http://www.aafp.org/afp/20030615/2517.html (Accessed January 28, 2006)

Center for Disease Control and Prevention. "Having a Healthy Pregnancy" (October 5, 2005). http://www.cdc.gov/ncbddd/bd/abc.htm (Accessed January 28, 2006)

Cohen, Philip. "Medical Journals to Require Clinical Trial Registration." NewScientist.com News Service (September 9, 2004) http://www.newscientist.com/article.ns?id=dn6378 (Accessed February 6, 2006)

Eisler, Peter, and Donna Leinwand. "Canada Top Source for Drug Chemical." *USA Today* (January 9, 2002). http://www.usatoday.com/news/nation/2002/ 01/10/usat-canada.htm (Accessed January 25, 2006)

Farmvillenc.com. "The Changing Landscape of Pharmaceutical Medicine" (2005). http://www.farmvillenc.com/the_changing_landscape.asp (Accessed February 6, 2006)

Graedon, Joe, and Teresa Graedon. *The People's Pharmacy*. New York: St. Martin's Press, 1998.

Griffith, H. Winter, and Stephen W. Moore. *Complete Guide To Prescription and Nonprescription Drugs*. New York: Perigree Trade Books, 2005.

Hingley, Audrey. "Preventing Childhood Poisoning" (June 1997). http://www.fda.gov/fdac/features/296_kid.html (accessed February 4, 2006)

Hirschhorn, Norbert, Robert Feldman, and Ian Greaves. "Abraham Lincoln's 'Blue Pills': Did our 16th President Suffer Mercury Intoxication?" *Perspectives in Biology and Medicine* (2001), Vol. 44, No.3:315–332. http://www.ncbi.nlm.nih.gov/entrez/query.fcgi?cmd=Retrieve &db= pubmed& dopt=Abstract&list_uids=11482002&query_hl=1 &itool=pubmed_docsum (Accessed January 30, 2006)

Janssen, Wallace F. "The Story Of The Laws Behind The Labels." *FDA Consumer* (June, 1981). http://www.cfsan.fda.gov/~lrd/history1.html#toc (Accessed January 25, 2006)

Larson, Anne, et al. "Acetaminophen-induced Acute Liver Failure: Results of a United States Multicenter, Prospective Study." *Hepatology* 42, no. 6 (December 2005):1364–1372. http://www.ncbi.nlm.nih.gov/entrez/query.fcgi?cmd=Retrieve&db=pubmed&d opt=Abstract&list_uids=16317692&query_hl=6&i tool=pubmed_docsum (Accessed February 2, 2006)

Leinwand, Donna. "Youths Risk Death in Latest Drug Abuse Trend." *USA Today* (December 29, 2003). http://www.usatoday.com/news/ health/2003-12-29-drug-abuse-cover_x.htm (Accessed February 9, 2006)

Manhart, M. D. "In Vitro Antimicrobial Activity of Bismuth Subsalicylate and Other Bismuth Salts." *Reviews of Infectious Diseases* 12 Suppl 1 (Jan–Feb 1990):S11-5. http://www.ncbi.nlm.nih.gov/entrez/query.fcgi?cmd=Retrieve&db=PubMed&list_uids=2406851&dopt=Abstract (Accessed February 9, 2006)

Mayo Clinic Staff. "Over the Counter Laxatives: Use Them with Caution" (April 29, 2005). http://www.mayoclinic.com/invoke.cfm?id=hq00088 (Accessed February 9, 2006)

McCoy, Bob "Overview: Great American Fraud." http://www.mtn.org/quack/ephemera/overview.htm (Accessed February 9, 2006)

MedicineNet.com. "Nonsteroidal Anti-inflammatory Drug." http://www.medterms.com/script/main/art.asp?articlekey=10380 (Accessed February 9, 2006)

The Museum of Questionable Medical Devices, http://www.mtn.org/quack/ephemera/dec0201.htm (Accessed Jan. 30, 2006)

Nordenberg, Tamar. "New Drug Label Spells It Out Simply." Federal Citizen Information Center. http://www.pueblo.gsa.gov/cic_text/health/newdrug-label/499_otc.html (Accessed January 29, 2006)

Ross-Flanigan, Nancy. "Antidiarrheal Drugs." Health AtoZ. http://www.healthatoz.com/healthatoz/

Atoz/ency/antidiarrheal_drugs.jsp (Accessed February 9, 2006)

The Thalidomide Society. "What is Thalidomide?" (2005). http://www.thalidomidesociety.co.uk/whatis.htm (Accessed February 9, 2006)

United States Food and Drug Administration. "How to Report Problems With Products Regulated by FDA" (March 29, 2005). http://www.fda.gov/opacom/ backgrounders/problem.html#products (Accessed February 9, 2006)

United States Food and Drug Administration. "Questions and Answers about FDA's Actions on Dietary Supplements Containing Ephedrine Alkaloids" (February 6, 2004). http://www.fda.gov/oc/initiatives/ephedra/february2004/qa_020 604.html (Accessed February 9, 2006)

United States Food and Drug Administration. "Safety of Phenylpropanolamine." Public Health Advisory, November 6, 2000. (Accessed January 28, 2006)

United States Food and Drug Administration, Center for Drug Evaluation and Research. "Health Hints: Use Caution with Pain Relievers" (January 22, 2004). http://www.fda.gov/cder/drug/analgesics/ healthHints.htm (Accessed February 9, 2006)

United States Food and Drug Administration, Center for Drug Evaluation and Research. "Kids Aren't Just Small Adults: Medicines, Children and the Care Every Child Deserves" (July 28, 2005). http://www.fda.gov/cder/consumerinfo/ kids.htm (Accessed February 9, 2006)

United States Food and Drug Administration, Center for Drug Evaluation and Research. "Over-the-Counter Medicines: What's Right for You?" (August 17, 2005). http://www.fda.gov/cder/ consumerinfo/WhatsRightForYou.htm (Accessed February 9, 2006)

United States Food and Drug Administration, Center for Drug Evaluation and Research. "The New Over-the-Counter Medicine Label: Take a Look" (August 17, 2005). http://www.fda.gov/cder/ consumerinfo/OTClabel.htm (Accessed February 9, 2006)

United States Food and Drug Administration, Center for Food Safety and Applied Nutrition. "Is It a Cosmetic, a Drug, or Both? (Or Is It Soap?)" (July 8, 2002). http://www.cfsan.fda.gov/~dms/ cos-218.html (Accessed February 9, 2006)

United States Food and Drug Administration. "Facts About Generic Drugs" (August 17, 2005). http://www.fda.gov/cder/consumerinfo/ generic_FactsAbout_text.htm (Accessed January 28, 2006)

Wikipedia. "Non-steroidal Anti-Inflammatory Drug." http://en.wikipedia.org/wiki/NSAID(Accessed February 9, 2006)

Wikipedia. "Patent Medicine." http://en.wikipedia. org/ wiki/Nostrum (Accessed February 9, 2006)

INDEX

ABOUT THE AUTHOR

Lorrie Klosterman, Ph.D., is a biologist and a freelance writer and educator. Her books for Marshall Cavendish Benchmark include *Leukemia, Meningitis, The Facts About Caffeine,* and *The Facts About Depressants.*

DATE DUE

OCT 2 1 2010			
OhioLINK			
OCT 2 4 2010			
GAYLORD			PRINTED IN U.S.A.